Little Hymns™

Little Hymns • Tell Me The Stories of Jesus
Written and illustrated by Andy Holmes
Watercolor by Cameron Thorp and Matt Taylor
Music transcription by Marty Franks

Copyright ©1992 by HSH Educational Media Company
P.O. Box 167187, Irving, Texas 75016

First Printing 1992
ISBN 0-929216-59-8
Printed in the United States of America

Published by

PRESS

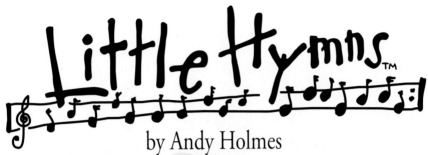

Little Hymns™

by Andy Holmes

Tell Me The Stories Of Jesus

Tell me the sto - ries of Je - sus

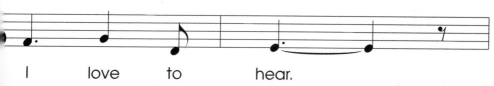

I love to hear.

Things I would ask Him to tell me if He were here.

Scenes   by   the   way - side,

Tales   of   the   sea,

Sto - ries of Je - sus,

Tell them to me.

Stood 'round His knee,

And I shall fan-cy His bless-ing rest-ing on me.

Words full of kind - ness,

Deeds full of grace,

All in the love - light of Je - sus' face!

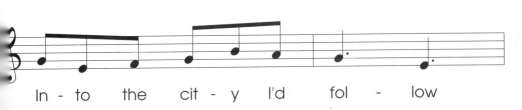

The chil - dren's band,

Wav-ing a branch of the palm tree high in my hand.

One   of   His   her - alds,

Yes,   I   would   sing

Loud - est ho - san - nas,

"Je - sus is King!"

Tell Me The Stories Of Jesus